BEANSTALKER

Edward Kenny

**A Story Based on "Jack and the Beanstalk," Told in Prose,
Dialogue and Verse for Young Readers of All Ages**

**Based on the Musical "Beanstalker"
By Val Angrosini (Music) and Edward Kenny (Book and Lyrics)**

Bluebird Publishing--Lindenhurst, NY
ISBN: 979-8-9859987-2-6
eBook ISBN: 979-8-3302-0636-0
Library of Congress Control Number:
Title: *Beanstalker*
Author: Edward Kenny
Available formats: eBook | paperback distribution

For further information, contact bluebirdsongspub@gmail.com

Published in the United States by New Book Authors Publishing

Dedication

For Aidan (Crash) and Harper (Hap).

Ever since he was a young boy in old England, "THE MAGICIAN" wanted to do magic. Even as an old man and he still wanted to be considered as a magician. In fact, that's what the people call him "the MAGICIAN." And yet, he never felt that they were being respectful. He knew they thought of him as someone whose tricks would backfire and whose spells would lead to disaster. But then, he had an idea. If he could do something magical to help someone, his skills would become famous throughout the land. And he could even make a profit in the process.

Alongside of a country road, there was a small farm. The farmer, whose name was RICHARD, was once a knight, but he grew tired of fighting battles, and choose instead to marry the love of his life, ANN, and to raise crops and animals on a farm. After RICHARD and ANN were married, they had a baby boy, who they named JACK.

JACK loved to play on the farm and he loved his father and mother. The family would have lived happily, but there was a wicked GIANT living above them in a castle in the sky. The GIANT was very mean and so was his wife, the GIANTESS. Having always wanting to be rich and beautiful, she became very wealthy because the GIANT stole gold and other valuable things from the people of the countryside. She did not become beautiful, but it didn't matter, because she was very conceited and thought that she was the prettiest thing in the sky.

The GIANT wanted to steal RICHARD's farm, but as big and powerful as he was, because he was a bully, he was actually also a coward. He was afraid of RICHARD because he was once a knight who was skilled in combat. So, the GIANT decided to force the MAGICIAN to cast a spell on RICHARD to weaken him. The MAGICIAN didn't know what to do. If he didn't obey the GIANT, he would hurt him, for he was an old man and could not well defend himself. But then, the MAGICIAN realized that he could trick the GIANT into thinking he was obeying him by casting only a minor spell on RICHARD. In so doing, he would also be helping RICHARD and his family. What a great idea! What a great magician people would say he was! Those were his thoughts.

And so, the MAGICIAN did cast the "minor" spell on RICHARD. Unfortunately, the spell was not minor at all. After he waved his wand, RICHARD disappeared in a puff of smoke. The GIANT took everything his family owned. He would also cast his large shadow over the farm so that nothing could grow there again.

In a way, the MAGICIAN was proud that he could do any magic trick at all, but he felt sad and guilty that ANN had lost her husband and that JACK had lost his father, and they were now very poor and starving.

The MAGICIAN tried and tried, but he could not reverse the spell. But perhaps he could help in some other way. With this in mind, he knocked on the door of their farmhouse and this is what happened.

MAGICIAN
Do you believe in magic?

ANN
I couldn't afford it if I did.

MAGICIAN
But I'm not selling anything.

ANN

Good. I'm not buying...

STORYTELLER

But the MAGICIAN blocked the door

MAGICIAN

I only want you to believe.

ANN

In what?

MAGICIAN

In yourself.

STORYTELLER

But she started to close the door again.

ANN

My "self" tells me you're a charlatan. You made my husband disappear and you said you can't bring him back. Goodbye.

STORYTELLER

So, he blocked the door again.

MAGICIAN

What if I believe I can pull a rabbit out of my pocket?

STORYTELLER

But, he accidentally pulled out flowers by mistake.

ANN

Remarkable. I'll thank you to be on your way, otherwise, I'll call the man of the house.

MAGICIAN

I see. Well now, that won't be necessary.

ANN

Magic, hymph!

STORYTELLER

And so, he left, saying:

MAGICIAN

Believe in yourself, that's the magic.

STORYTELLER

As he walked away, he could see JACK, coming beside ANN in the doorway. This is what they said:

JACK

Mother, I'll send him packing.

ANN

Easy dear, he's leaving under his own power.

JACK

It's a good thing for him.

ANN

Now, JACK, you're still just a boy.

JACK

But you said so yourself...I'm the man of the house.

ANN

That was to scare him away.

JACK

It was?

ANN

Yes. And it would have been more effective had you stayed out of view.

STORYTELLER

ANN realized that she is deflating his spirit, so she hugged him as she said:

ANN

But you will be a fine strapping man one day like…

JACK

Like my father was?

ANN

Oh, if only he were here to see you.

JACK

And to put food on our table...Tell me again, Mother...

ANN

Tell you what?

JACK

About our life before...when we weren't poor. About, you know...

STORYTELLER
And ANN said:

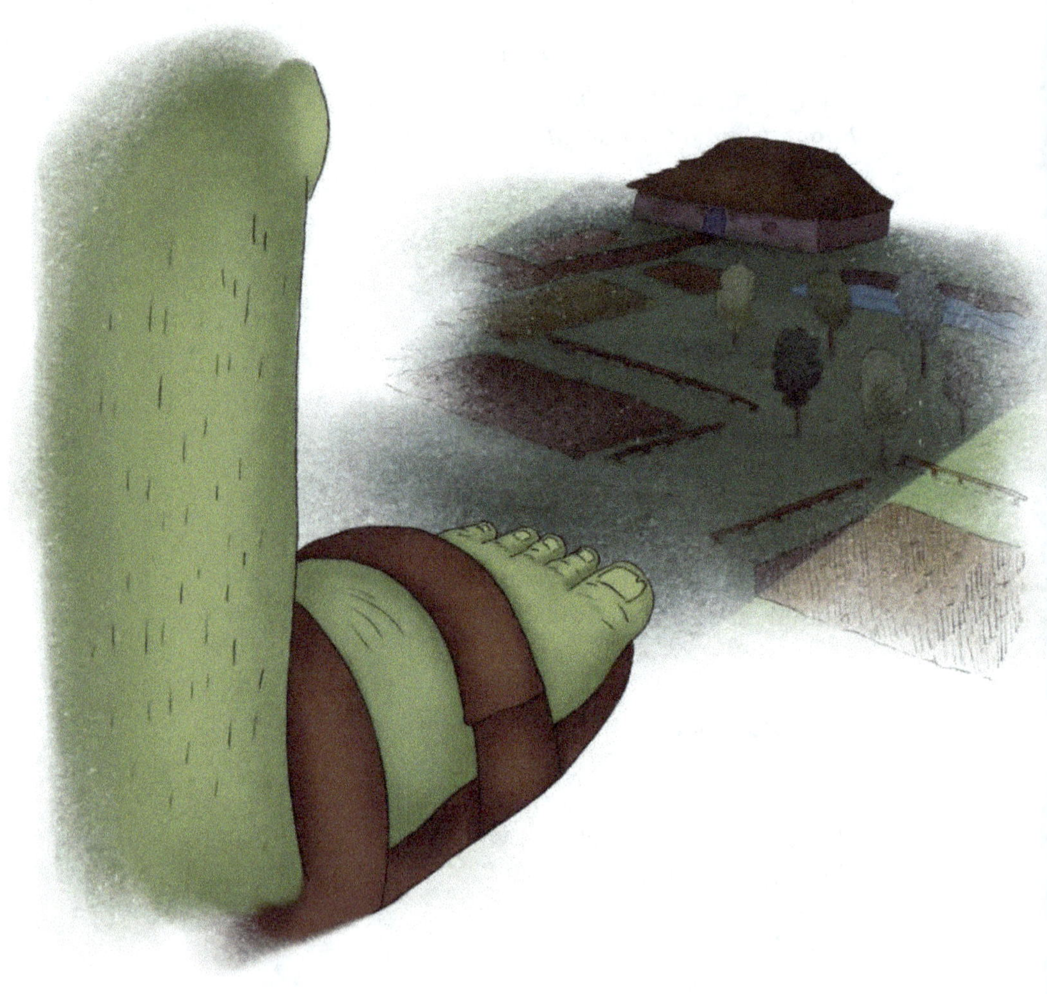

ANN

ONCE UPON A TIME WHEN I WAS YOUNG,
WHEN BIRDS WERE ALWAYS SINGING,
IT IS TO THE SONGS THAT THEY HAVE
SUNG, AND TO MEMORIES I'M CLINGING.

FOR IT WAS THE SPRINGTIME OF OUR
LIVES,
AND IT SHOULD HAVE BEEN FOREVER,
WITH A LINK BETWEEN HUSBANDS AND
WIVES,
IN A CHAIN NO ONE COULD SEVER.

BUT THEN A SHADOW CAME ACROSS THE
LAND
AND CRUSHED THE MOUNTAINS OF OUR
DREAMS TO SAND.
THEN, AS IN AN ECLIPSE, WE LOST THE
SUN,
AND SOON OUR ONCE UPON A TIME WAS
DONE.

ONCE UPON A TIME THERE WAS A FARM,
AND ON IT LIVED A FAMILY.
BUT ONLY TWO WOULD BE SAVED FROM
HARM,
JUST A MOTHER AND HER BABY.

NOW I PONDER ALL THE WINTER NIGHT,
AS THE LONGEST PATH I TRAVEL,
HOW THE TAPESTRY ONCE IN MY SIGHT
WAS SO QUICKLY TO UNRAVEL.

JUST WHEN A SHADOW CAME ACROSS THE
LAND,
AND CRUSHED THE MOUNTAINS OF OUR
DREAMS TO SAND.
THEN, AS IN AN ECLIPSE, WE LOST THE
SUN,

9

AND SOON OUR ONCE UPON A TIME WAS
DONE.

                    STORYTELLER
Then JACK said:

                       JACK
ONCE UPON A TIME THERE WAS A MAN,
AND HE WATCHED WHILE I WAS SLEEPING.
I KNOW HE WATCHED OVER ME AND
SMILED,
I WAS SAFELY WITHIN HIS KEEPING.

                    STORYTELLER
*Then JACK imagined RICHARD was with him and
saying:*

                      RICHARD
IN A FAIRY TALE I WAS A KNIGHT,
AND I LOVED WITHOUT PRETENDING,
NOW I WANDER THROUGH AN ENDLESS
NIGHT,
IN SEARCH OF A HAPPY ENDING.

                    STORYTELLER
*Before long, the image of RICHARD in JACK's
mind disappeared and ANN and JACK said:*

                   ANN AND JACK
ONE DAY A LIGHT WILL SHINE ACROSS THE
LAND,
AND WE'LL BUILD MOUNTAINS OUT OF
DREAMS AND SAND.
THEN, AS COLORS SPARKLE AFTER THE
RAIN,
WE'LL HAVE OUR ONCE UPON A TIME
AGAIN.

STORYTELLER
Suddenly, a shadow covered the farm. JACK said:

JACK
Mother! There it is! The shadow that crossed the land. It was him, wasn't it?

STORYTELLER
JACKs mother pretended not to know that the shadow was cast by the GIANT because she didn't want to alarm JACK.

ANN
Who?

JACK
Oh, you know, the GIANT. He changed our life. He took my father away.

ANN
Now, Jack, it wasn't that simple. There was a spell cast by a magician.

STORYTELLER
Then she held him in her arms, but he wanted to break free as he heard the GIANT's loud voice thundering these words:

GIANT
WHEN MY STOMACH GRUMBLES,
I ONLY WANT TO EAT.
AND I'M NOT TOO CONCERNED WITH
WHO'S BELOW MY FEET.

SQUISH GO LITTLE HOUSES,
CRUSHED BELOW ME LIKE TOYS.
I SEND PEOPLE RUNNING,
AND SNATCH UP GIRLS AND BOYS.

BUT I'M JUST YOUR AVERAGE BIG GUY,
AND THERE IS ONE IN EVERY TOWN,
AND THEY SAY I'M CONDESCENDING,
BUT I'M ONLY LOOKING DOWN.

STORYTELLER
*Despite his mother's disapproval, JACK shouted up
to the GIANT defiantly:*

JACK
YES, HE'S JUST YOUR AVERAGE BIG GUY
WHO SHOULD STAND INSIDE OUR SHOES.

STORYTELLER
The GIANT shouted back to JACK.

GIANT
I WOULD, BUT I'M SIZE FIFTY-EIGHT,
AND YOU ALL WEAR ONES AND TWOS.

THERE'S NOTHING THAT HUMBLES
MY EGO'S HEARTY HEALTH,
YET, I'M STILL UNSELFISH,
I'M QUICK TO SHARE THE WEALTH.

I DROP LITTLE MORSELS
ON ANYONE WHO BEGS.

STORYTELLER
ANN covered her mouth as she spoke to JACK

ANN
BUT HE WON'T BE SHARING,
HIS GOOSE'S GOLDEN EGGS.

YES, HE'S YOUR AVERAGE BIG GUY
WHO SHOULD SEE OUR POINT OF VIEW.

STORYTELLER
Then they spoke back and forth.

GIANT
I WOULD, BUT I'M MY OWN HERO,
I'VE NO ONE TO LOOK UP TO.

AND I'M JUST YOUR AVERAGE BIG GUY,
JUST YOUR AVERAGE EXTRA-LARGE.

ANN
HE SHOULD SAIL UPON OUR BOAT.

JACK
IT WOULD HAVE TO BE A BARGE.

ANN
OFF AGAIN HE RUMBLES WHILE WE LIE IN
DEFEAT.

JACK
STILL, I'M NOT CONVINCED,
THAT HE CANNOT BE BEAT.

LIKE A TALL TREE STANDING
HIGH ABOVE OUR HUTS,
WE HAVE GOT THE AXES...

GIANT
HAVE YOU GOT THE GUTS?

YES, I'M JUST YOUR AVERAGE BIG GUY,
WHOSE HEAD IS IN THE MIST,
AND A NEIGHBOR WHO IS PEACEFUL,
I ONLY WANT TO CO-EXIST.

JACK
NO, HE'S NOT YOUR AVERAGE BIG GUY,
A BULLY AND BRUTE.
AND IT'S TIME TO PUT OUR FOOT UP,
AND GIVE HIM THE BOOT.

STORYTELLER
After the GIANT left, ANN spoke to JACK.

ANN
Jack, we must do something or we will surely
starve.

JACK
Why?

ANN
The shadow of the GIANT has robbed our crops of
the sunlight.

JACK
I suppose I'm not the man of the house after all. If I
were, I'd think of something.

ANN
Never mind about that now. I have an idea of how
you can help.

JACK
Really? How?

ANN
By selling the only valuable possession we have
left.

JACK
Not the house.

ANN
No, for if we did we would freeze.

JACK

Then what?

ANN

Our cow.

JACK

Oh, but Mother, she is like one of the family...and we are a small family.

ANN

Really? Do you think she resembles me?

JACK

Perhaps a little…er, I mean, no, but you know what I mean.

ANN

I do, but nevertheless, you must sell her so that we can preserve our family and our home.

JACK

But...

ANN

Just take her to market before I change my mind. Go.

JACK

But...

ANN

Be my little man!

JACK

Oh, all right, I will.

STORYTELLER

So, JACK went on his way. He followed a road that led through the forest to the village where the market was located. He was leading the family cow along the road where the MAGICIAN stepped in again to "help." JACK didn't seem to know who he was as he spoke to him, saying...

MAGICIAN

Do you believe in magic?

JACK

I don't talk with strangers.

MAGICIAN

But I'm no stranger. I was at your house today.

JACK

And it's a good thing you left when you did.

MAGICIAN

Indeed, for you must be the man of the house.

JACK

That I am!

MAGICIAN

And this?

JACK

Is our cow, or was our cow.

MAGICIAN

Was?

JACK

I'm taking her to market. Now, if you'll excuse me,
technically, you are still a stranger.

MAGICIAN

Yes, but this morning, you never got to see me do
my tricks.

JACK

You mean the rabbit that never appeared?

MAGICIAN

Oh, I see, a doubter.

JACK

A doubter?

MAGICIAN

One who does not believe in magic.

JACK

If I saw some, perhaps I'd believe.

MAGICIAN

Then allow me to amaze you.

JACK

Not the rabbit trick again.

MAGICIAN

Not at all! Stand back, lest you be burned by fire!

STORYTELLER

*At that the MAGICIAN reached into his pocket, again
thinking he could produce a torch. Instead, the same flowers
he produced earlier, once again appeared by mistake. Then,
JACK said sarcastically...*

JACK

So, that's what causes forest fires...Flowers.

STORYTELLER

The MAGICIAN was dejected, but as JACK turned to leave, he called to him saying:

MAGICIAN

Wait! Perhaps I'm not the world's greatest magician...

JACK

That's all right, but maybe you should just say that you'll make flowers appear...that always works.

MAGICIAN

Very funny. But let's be serious for a moment, JACK.

STORYTELLER

And our conversation continued:

JACK

I really shouldn't be talking to a stranger.

MAGICIAN

That's just the point. JACK, I know, I mean, I knew your father.

JACK

You did? Tell me what happened to him.

MAGICIAN

I can't.

JACK

But why?

MAGICIAN

Not yet.

JACK

Not yet? But when? What do you mean?

MAGICIAN

I feel a certain responsibility to help you and your mother.

JACK

Mother mentioned a magician...was it you?

MAGICIAN

Let me help you, JACK.

JACK

How do you know my name?

STORYTELLER

The MAGICIAN thought that it was time for him to get stern with JACK.

MAGICIAN

No more questions.

JACK

But, my father...

MAGICIAN

Right now, you and your mother need food or you'll starve.

JACK

Then I must go and sell this cow.

MAGICIAN

I'll buy it.

JACK

You will? For how much?

STORYTELLER
The MAGICIAN held out his hand. In it were some beans...beans that the MAGICIAN thought would magically yield many crops of fruits and vegetables that ANN and JACK could sell for a profit. He said...

MAGICIAN
This much.

JACK
But they're beans.

MAGICIAN
Magic beans!

JACK
Are they going to turn into flowers? Or hot air? You know...beans?

MAGICIAN
They will yield a bounty of food.

JACK
I, I don't know about this.

STORYTELLER
The MAGICIAN wrapped the beans in my fist and began to walk away, saying:

MAGICIAN
Then I'll be on my way.

JACK
Well, a cow should be sold for twenty shillings.

MAGICIAN
No, that's not the best price. Don't be a fool, Jack. Let me tell you why...

MAGICIAN
A LAD WHO IS OFF FOR THE CITY,
MUST CHOOSE THE APPROPRIATE TRAIL.
THEY ALL PAINT A PICTURE SO PRETTY,
BUT SOME WILL STILL LEAD YOU TO FAIL.

A LAD IS IN NEED OF A MENTOR,
WITH A WEALTH OF KNOWLEDGE TO SHARE.
IT'S ALL ABOUT CAVEAT EMPTOR,
YOU KNOW, LET THE BUYER BEWARE.

A LAD WHO IS FULL OF AMBITION,
WHO'LL RISK EVERYTHING HE MIGHT OWN,
CAN IMPROVE HIS PRESENT CONDITION
AS FAST AS A SEED CAN BE SOWN.

JACK
BUT WHAT PRICE WOULD YOU HAVE ME
PAYING
TO POSSESS A NOBLEMAN'S MEANS?

MAGICIAN
ARE YOU DEAF TO ALL I'VE BEEN SAYING?
CAN'T YOU SEE THAT IT GOES FOR BEANS?

IT'S A PROSPEROUS DAY IN THE FOREST,
WHEN A MEETING OF MERCHANTS
CONVENES.
I CAN STACK UP A GIANT TRANSACTION,
AND THEN INFLUENCE WHICH WAY IT
LEANS.
AND BELIEVE ME IT'S WORTH IT,
ONCE YOU UNEARTH IT,
IT GOES FOR BEANS.

MY PRODUCT, YOU SEE, IS ENCHANTED,
TOMORROW YOU'LL UNDERSTAND HOW.
REMEMBER THE IDEAS I'VE PLANTED
AND LET GO OF YOUR SACRED COW.

WHAT GOOD IS AN ASSET THAT'S FROZEN?
YOU'VE TRADED FOR SOMETHING THAT
GROWS.

STORYTELLER
*With that, JACK took the beans and handed over the cow to
the MAGICIAN. He wouldn't have taken the cow, but he
thought he had a trick to turn it into an entire herd.
Unfortunately, that didn't work either. In any event, JACK
and the MAGICIAN closed the deal saying:*

JACK
WILL MY MOTHER LIKE WHAT I HAVE CHOSEN?

MAGICIAN
OUR DEALINGS HAVE COME TO A CLOSE.

MAGICIAN
IT'S A PROSPEROUS WAY TO DO BUSINESS
WHEN A STROKE OF GOOD LUCK
INTERVENES,
A CUSTOMER RIPE FOR THE PICKING,
LIKE THIS LAD CAN BE PULLED FROM THE
GREENS.
AND WHILE HE'S UNASSUMING,
PROFIT IS BOOMING.
IT GOES FOR BEANS.

STORYTELLER
*When JACK returned home, his mother greeted him
saying:*

ANN

Tell me, my man of the house, how much did our cow bring? Fifteen? Twenty?

STORYTELLER

Sheepishly, JACK answered.

JACK

No.

STORYTELLER

ANN became concerned as they spoke further, saying:

ANN

How much then?

JACK

Oh, five, or six...

ANN

Only five or six shillings?

JACK

Not exactly.

ANN

JACK, did you sell our cow?

JACK

Oh, yes.

ANN

For what?

JACK

Beans.

ANN

Beans?

JACK

Magic beans!

ANN

Oh, Jack...You met that MAGICIAN and you were
swindled, weren't you?

JACK

But Mother, they're magical! They can bring us
food and news...

ANN

News?

JACK

About Father.

ANN

Oh, poor JACK, that good-for-nothing MAGICIAN
played upon your emotions.

JACK

But Mother, he knew Father.

ANN

Of course. It was he that put a curse on him...that's
how he disappeared.

STORYTELLER
JACK became angry and said:

JACK

Then I will go after him.

STORYTELLER
ANN held him back, saying:

ANN

No! No, Jack. You saw how his tricks backfire.

JACK

But you said he cast a curse on Father.

ANN

It was the GIANT who ordered the curse. The MAGICIAN tried to cast a harmless spell, he just miscalculated the dosage and your father disappeared in a puff of smoke.

JACK

But, he wanted to help us now.

ANN

I know he wants to help, but I think he's "helped" enough. Give me the beans.

STORYTELLER

JACK handed ANN the beans and she tossed them into their garden, as she said:

ANN

They'll come to no good.

STORYTELLER

Because JACK was feeling guilty and low, he said:

JACK

I'm sorry, Mother, I ruined everything. I let you down as the man of the house.

STORYTELLER

ANN consoled him, saying:

ANN

Never you mind. The MAGICIAN was right about one thing.

JACK

What's that?

ANN

Real magic comes from believing in yourself. Don't lose your confidence. Our luck will change.

JACK

Until it does, I suppose we'll have no dinner again.

ANN

I'm sorry for that.

JACK

It's all right, Mother, I'm too tired to eat. Good night.

STORYTELLER

ANN kissed him goodnight.

ANN

Good night my brave boy.

STORYTELLER

JACK went to bed. During the night, while he and ANN were sleeping, something happened. JACK woke early the next morning. He glanced out of the window and did a double take. He couldn't believe what he saw. A beanstalk was rising far above the house, only to disappear into the clouds above. JACK ran to look out the window. Next, he ran through the doorway of the house to the beanstalk, shouting at first, then speaking just above a whisper, saying:

JACK

Mother, look! See, I told you. The beans were magical.

STORYTELLER

She did not hear, so he continued, saying:

JACK

But where can it lead? I cannot ask permission. If Mother says no, I cannot disobey. But if don't ask, I must believe in myself.

STORYTELLER

JACK began to climb the beanstalk, saying:

JACK

I must climb to the highest place I can reach.

STORYTELLER

As he climbed, he spoke his thoughts out loud, saying:

JACK

WAITING, STALLING
THINKING ABOUT FALLING.
RISING HIGHER,
MOVED BY SHEER DESIRE.
TWISTING, TURNING,
STEP BY STEP I'M LEARNING.
OVER UNDER,
ALL THE WORLD ASUNDER.

AND I'M VOWING NOT TO STOP,
UNTIL I REACH THE TOP.
WHERE I'LL TOUCH THE ANGELS' SHROUDS,
ABOVE MY LADDER THROUGH THE CLOUDS.

AND THERE'S A WORLD,
I'VE BEEN TOLD,
UP IN THE SKY,
WHERE ALL YOU NEED,
IS TO LOVE,
AND YOU CAN FLY.
FOR IT'S A PLACE IN BETWEEN REASON
AND RHYME,
IT'S A PLACE I LIVED IN ONCE UPON A TIME.

PULLING, CLIMBING,
DEVELOPING TIMING.
FASTER, STRONGER,
NO FEAR ANY LONGER.
BOBBING, WEAVING,
SINCERELY BELIEVING,
GROWING, GLOWING,
LIKE A TREE OF KNOWING.

I REFUSE TO SEE THE SIGHTS,
SO FEARFUL OF THE HEIGHTS,
LOST BY FOLLOWING THE CROWDS,
BELOW MY LADDER THROUGH THE CLOUDS.

AND I COULD SWEAR,
THERE'S A SPIRIT,
WHO HAS SMILED,
HIS IS A FACE I REMEMBER,
AS A CHILD,
BACK IN A HOME WHERE OUR LIFE WAS
ALWAYS SO SUBLIME,
IT'S A PLACE I LIVED IN ONCE UPON A TIME.

STORYTELLER

As he continued climbing up the beanstalk, JACK disappeared into the clouds. There he met a young girl, named MELODY, who was dressed like a fairy, and who was perhaps a year or two older than Jack. JACK spoke to her saying:

JACK

Hello, I'm Jack. Who are you?

STORYTELLER

MELODY laughed playfully and started to fly all around him. Then she spoke these words:

MELODY

I COULD TELL YOU IN WORDS,
BUT THAT WOULD BE SOMETHING LESS
THAN THE SUM OF THE FEELINGS,
THAT MY MOVEMENTS EXPRESS.

THEY TAKE ME TO A PLACE,
THAT NO MORTAL HAS YET SEEN,
NOT ON EARTH, OR IN HEAVEN,
BUT SOMEPLACE IN BETWEEN.

WHERE I CAN FLY,
WHERE I CAN SOAR,
WHERE THERE'S A WINDOW IN THE SKY,
WHERE THERE'S NO CEILING AND NO FLOOR.

WHERE IF YOU WILL,
JUST TAKE A CHANCE,
WE'LL STEP UPON A WINDOWSILL,
AND JUMP OFF TO WHERE SPIRITS DANCE.

PAST THE GATES OF THE CLOUDS,
SHINES THE LIGHT YOU'VE BEEN DENIED.

STORYTELLER
*Then, slowly landing next to him, she took JACK's
hand. At first, he hesitated, then he joined her, flying
through the clouds. Then they spoke to each other,
saying:*

JACK
I'M AFRAID I'LL LOSE MYSELF
IF I SHOULD PEER INSIDE.

MELODY
IN EACH LIFE A TIME COMES TO,
REACH OUT TO TOUCH OUR DREAMS,
THOUGH THEY SEEM IN THE DISTANCE,
THEY'RE CLOSER THAN IT SEEMS.

JACK AND MELODY
WHERE WE CAN FLY,
WHERE WE CAN SOAR,
WHERE THERE'S A WINDOW IN THE SKY,
WHERE THERE'S NO CEILING AND NO
FLOOR.

WHERE IF WE WILL
JUST TAKE A CHANCE,
WE'LL STEP UPON A WINDOWSILL,
AND JUMP OFF TO WHERE SPIRITS DANCE.

JACK
YOU CAN SEE IN MY EYES,
WHILE YOU PERFORM YOUR ART,
LIKE THE WINGS OF AN ANGEL,
YOU HAVE OPENED MY HEART.

WHITE VAPOR IN THE BLUE,
I WATCH YOUR WINDSWEPT BALLET,

AND STILL REMAINS YOUR IMAGE,
WHEN YOU'VE FLOATED AWAY.

STORYTELLER
She led him back to his perch on the beanstalk and they continued to speak.

JACK AND MELODY
WHERE WE CAN FLY,
WHERE WE CAN SOAR,
WHERE THERE'S A WINDOW IN THE SKY,
WHERE THERE'S A CEILING AND NO FLOOR.

WHERE IF WE WILL
JUST TAKE THE CHANCE,
WE'LL STEP UPON A WINDOWSILL,
AND JUMP OFF TO WHERE SPIRITS DANCE.

STORYTELLER
Slowly, MELODY began to fade away into the clouds, and JACK called out:

JACK
Wait! I don't even know your name.

MELODY
It's MELODY.

JACK
Won't you stay and teach me to fly, to be free like you are?

MELODY
But I am not free. I am the slave of the Master.

JACK
The Master?

MELODY

The GIANT. What you see is only my spirit. The part of me he can't imprison in a harp to sing whenever he commands it.

JACK

But I will set you free. It's time I met this GIANT. We have a score to settle.

MELODY

No, JACK. He is too big and strong and you are just a boy.

JACK

But I'm not! I'm a man. You'll see.

STORYTELLER

She continued to fade away, becoming invisible, as JACK shouted:

JACK

MELODY, wait!

STORYTELLER

She had disappeared, but JACK could hear her voice saying:

MELODY

I cannot stay. For my spirit grows weak anytime it leaves my body for too long.

STORYTELLER

They continued to speak, with him in the flesh and her as only a voice.

JACK

But I wish to save you. Tell me how I can help.

MELODY

Don't try. Climb back down the beanstalk.

JACK

But you said I could find that place where spirits fly. Where is that place?

MELODY

Up above. But you must not go there. Goodbye.

JACK

Wait! I must keep climbing.

STORYTELLER

With that, MELODY was gone, but true to his word, JACK did keep on climbing. Eventually, he reached the top of the beanstalk, just above the clouds. He walked upon the clouds a while, coming to a large doorway which was the entrance to the GIANT's castle. He stood before the door, where there was a huge door knocker. He was able to jump up and move the knocker, as he called out...

JACK

MELODY, are you in there? MELODY?

STORYTELLER

Standing immediately behind the door, it was not MELODY, but the GIANTESS, who responded:

GIANTESS

Just a moment. Who is calling?

JACK

I'm JACK. Is that you MELODY?

GIANTESS

Is MELODY a mere slip of a girl?

42

                          JACK

Yes.

                        GIANTESS

Is she beautiful?

                          JACK

Yes.

                        GIANTESS

Is she in the prime of her youth?

                       STORYTELLER

*Something was not right. JACK became suspicious.
He said:*

                          JACK

Yes.

                       STORYTELLER

*The GIANTESS swung the door open, looking to JACK as the
exact opposite of MELODY. The GIANTESS said:*

                        GIANTESS

Young, beautiful, who needs MELODY when you
have me?

                       STORYTELLER

*The GIANTESS was disappointed that JACK was as
young as he was.*

                        GIANTESS

Oh, but you are just a boy.

                       STORYTELLER

Backing away, JACK said:

JACK
I'm a man...but never mind, I must have the wrong
castle.

STORYTELLER
The GIANTESS held JACK by his shirt, saying:

GIANTESS
HERE'S A LITTLE BOY...
I'LL CATCH HIM UNAWARE...
SUCH A PRECIOUS TOY...
THE ANSWER TO MY PRAYER...

COME ALONG INSIDE
AND HAVE A LITTLE SNACK,
NO REASON TO HIDE,
UNTIL THE MASTER'S BACK.

STORYTELLER
JACK was looking for a way to escape.

JACK
No thank you, I'm looking for—

STORYTELLER
The GIANTESS grabbed JACK's arm saying:

GIANTESS
MELODY, why, of course. Well, she lives here.

STORYTELLER
*Then she took his arm and forced him toward the
back of the house, saying*

GIANTESS
Right this way.

STORYTELLER
*JACK saw humongous crumbs on the floor in the
kitchen where they conversed:*

GIANTESS
HAVE YOU NEVER SEEN
SUCH A LOVELY GIANTESS?
SUCH A BEAUT I MEAN,
GO AHEAD CONFESS.

JACK
NO, I'VE NEVER SEEN
THIS KIND OF GIANTESS.
SUCH A BEAUT, I MEAN
A BEAUTY OF A MESS.

BOULDERS ON THE FLOOR...

GIANTESS
OH, THEY'RE ONLY CRUMBS...

STORYTELLER
*JACK could hear the footsteps of the GIANT approaching.
He ran for the door, saying:*

JACK
LET ME OUT THE DOOR.

STORYTELLER
*She begins to hide JACK in the cupboard, but then
changed her mind.*

GIANTESS
TOO LATE, NOW HERE HE COMES,

BETTER PUT YOU IN THE CUPBOARD,
OH, NO, HE'LL LOOK IN THERE.
MAYBE THERE INSIDE THE CLOSET,
OH, NO, HE'LL SMELL YOU HERE.

STORYTELLER
Seeing no other option, the GIANTESS hid JACK behind her.

GIANTESS
QUICK, HERE, HIDE BEHIND ME,
JUST HOPE HE DOESN'T SEE,
THAT YOU'RE HERE TO SAVE ME,
FROM ALL THIS DRUDGERY.

STORYTELLER
Then, with footsteps that shook the entire house, the GIANT walked toward them. Nervously, the GIANTESS tried to make him doubt his senses.

GIANTESS
TAKE ANOTHER SNIFF,
THERE'S NO WAY IT COULD BE.
IT'S A PROBLEM WITH,
YOUR SENSE OLFACTORY.

GIANT
GO AND COOK MY FOOD,
NOW, ISN'T THAT YOUR JOB?

STORYTELLER
Then the GIANT left the room and the GIANTESS spoke to JACK. Saying:

                    GIANTESS
HE IS ALWAYS RUDE
AND ACTING LIKE A SLOB.

SOON IT ALL WILL END,
SO LONG AS YOU BEHAVE.
NOW YOU NEED A FRIEND,
AND NOW I NEED A SLAVE.

                    STORYTELLER
*And the GIANTESS handed JACK a broom that fit
his size, he began to sweep, saying to himself:*

                      JACK
I WILL MEET MY DOOM
IF I MAKE A PEEP.
I'LL PICK UP THE BROOM,
TO SURVIVE I'LL SWEEP...

CEILING TO THE FLOOR...

                    GIANTESS
UNDERNEATH MY THUMBS...

                   STORYTELLER
*JACK heard the GIANT coming back again. He
dropped the broom and ran for the door, saying:*

                      JACK
LET ME OUT THE DOOR!

                   STORYTELLER
But the GIANTESS grabbed him by the arm, saying:

BUM—
BUM

GIANTESS
TOO LATE, NOW HERE HE COMES.

STORYTELLER
She pushed JACK under the kitchen table, saying:

GIANTESS
BETTER HIDE UNDER THE TABLE.
OH, NO, HE'LL KICK YOU THERE.
MAYBE HERE, INSIDE THE BREAD BOX,
GOOD GRIEF, HE'LL EAT YOU THERE.

STORYTELLER
Again out of options, she pushed him behind her.

GIANTESS
AGAIN, HIDE BEHIND ME.

JACK
THAT'S SURE TO COVER ME...

STORYTELLER
Then they both said:

GIANTESS AND JACK
I CAN'T WAIT 'TIL I'M FREE
FROM ALL THIS DRUDGERY.

STORYTELLER
*The GIANT began peering around the room, suspecting that
something as was amiss. The GIANTESS escorted the GIANT
to his seat at the kitchen table to stop him from looking
around for JACK. She then backed JACK out of the room. As
she pushed JACK out of the room, the GIANT bellowed:*

GIANT
Woman! Why aren't you cooking my dinner?

STORYTELLER
As she walked back to the table, they argued:

GIANTESS
I DON'T LIKE COOKING,

GIANT
IT'S TIME TO EAT!

GIANTESS
(Under her breath.)
HE'S GARGANTUAN,

GIANT
(Under his breath.)
SHE'S SO PETITE.

GIANTESS
I'M A ROMANTIC.

GIANT
AND I'M A PRINCE.

GIANTESS
SO, MIRROR, WHO'S FAIRER?

GIANT
MIRROR, DON'T WINCE.

                    GIANTESS
HE LOOKS AT PICTURES,

                     GIANT
SHE'D RATHER READ.

                    GIANTESS
I DON'T GET FLOWERS...

                   STORYTELLER
*Then the GIANT handed her a sesame seed from a
piece of bread, saying:*

                     GIANT
HERE, HAVE A SEED.

              GIANT AND GIANTESS
THERE'S SOMEONE FOR EVERYONE,
THAT'S AN OBVIOUS FACT,
THERE'S SOMEONE FOR EVERYONE
AND OPPOSITES ATTRACT.

                     GIANT
I'M GOOD FOR HER...

                    GIANTESS
I'M GOOD FOR HIM.

                     GIANT
SO, I'M TOO TALL...

                    GIANTESS
SO, I'M TOO SLIM...

                     BOTH
WE'VE GOT NOTHING IN COMMON,
ON THAT WE ARE AGREED.
THERE'S SOMEONE FOR EVERYONE
AND WE'RE ALL THAT WE NEED.

GIANTESS
SO MANY SUITORS
CAME TO MY DOOR....

GIANT
THEY GOT A GOOD LOOK,
AND FELL TO THE FLOOR.

SO MANY DAMSELS,
I SAVE FROM DEATH.

GIANTESS
BUT THEY CHOOSE THE DRAGON,
OVER YOUR BREATH.

I WANTED SOMEONE,
SOMEONE LIKE ME.

GIANT
THERE'RE NOT MANY OTHERS
TALL AS A TREE.

I GUESS I'M LUCKY,

GIANTESS
COULD HAVE BEEN WORSE...

GIANT
THERE'S FOOD IN MY BELLY,

GIANTESS
GOLD IN MY PURSE.

BOTH
THERE'S SOMEONE FOR EVERYONE,
THAT'S AN OBVIOUS FACT.
THERE'S SOMEONE FOR EVERYONE,
AND OPPOSITES ATTRACT.

GIANT
I'M JUST HER TYPE,

GIANTESS
I'M A GOOD CATCH.

GIANT
SO, WHAT IF WE'RE NOT...

GIANTESS
THE PERFECT MATCH.

BOTH
WE'VE GOT NOTHING IN COMMON,
ON THAT WE'RE AGREED.
THERE'S SOMEONE FOR EVERYONE,
AND WE'RE ALL THAT WE NEED.

GIANT
I HAVE DEFEATED,
ALL OF MY FOES.

GIANTESS
CAUSE HE TRAPPED THEM,
BETWEEN HIS TOES.

I'M ON THE LEFT SIDE...

GIANT
I'M ON THE RIGHT,

STORYTELLER
*The mood of the GIANT and the GIANTESS became
lighter and they embraced and spoke to each other.*

GIANTESS
MEET IN THE MIDDLE...

GIANT
AT THE RIGHT HEIGHT.

BOTH
THERE'S SOMEONE FOR EVERYONE,
THAT'S AN OBVIOUS FACT.
THERE'S SOMEONE FOR EVERYONE,
AND OPPOSITES ATTRACT,
WE'VE GOT NOTHING IN COMMON,
ON THAT WE'RE AGREED.
THERE'S SOMEONE FOR EVERYONE
AND WE'RE ALL THAT WE NEED.

STORYTELLER
Meanwhile, down on the farm below, at the foot of the beanstalk a FARMER and his WIFE approached ANN, who was looking up at the massive plant. The FARMER said to ANN...

FARMER
Is it true that Jack climbed this beanstalk?

ANN
It is.

STORYTELLER
The FARMER said:

FARMER
Why would he try such a foolish thing?

ANN
I just wish he'd come back down. But, I'll tell you why he would go up there.

SOMEBODY'S GOT TO ASK THE QUESTION,
SOMEBODY'S GOT TO TAKE A STAND.
SOMEBODY'S GOT TO HAVE AN ANSWER,
SOMEBODY'S GOT TO RAISE THEIR HAND.
SOMEBODY'S STARTING AT THE BOTTOM,
ONE DAY, WHO'S BOUND TO REACH THE
TOP.
SOMEBODY'S PICKING UP MOMENTUM,
SOMEBODY NO ONE'S GOING TO STOP.

                    FARMER
SOMEBODY'S GOT TO BE A WINNER,
SOMEBODY ELSE WILL HAVE TO LOSE.
SOMEBODY'S GOT THAT LUCKY NUMBER,
AND THE WORLD IS FILLED WITH NUMBER
TWOS.

                  STORYTELLER
Then the FARMER'S WIFE said:

                FARMER'S WIFE
All the townspeople say he's going to try to slay the
GIANT.

                  STORYTELLER
ANN replied:

                      ANN
SOMEBODY'S GOT TO FACE THE GIANT,
ONE DAY, WHO'S BOUND TO BRING HIM DOWN.
IT'S JUST LIKE DAVID AND GOLIATH,
SAME STORY IN A DIFFERENT TOWN.

                  STORYTELLER
And they all said:

ALL
AND EVERYBODY LOOKS UP TO THE SKY,
SAYING WHO'S THAT CRAZY BOY ABOUT
TO DIE?
BEANSTALKER.
BUT HE MIGHT JUST SURPRISE US ALL AND
FLY,
'CAUSE HE'S THE BEANSTALKER,
NOT SOME OTHER GUY.
BEANSTALKER.

STORYTELLER
Unseen by the others, RICHARD appeared as a phantom, saying:

RICHARD
SOMEBODY'S GOT TO HAVE THE COURAGE
THAT GROWS FROM CONQUERING A FEAR.
SOMEBODY MUST BELIEVE IN SOMETHING,
AND RECOGNIZE IT WHEN IT'S THERE.

STORYTELLER
ANN continued:

ANN
SOMEBODY'S GOT TO BE A LONER,
BUT NO ONE DOES IT ALL ALONE.
TOGETHER, WE CAN CLIMB FOREVER,
DIVIDED, FALL JUST LIKE A STONE.

STORYTELLER
The others joined in saying:

                    ALL
AND EVERYBODY LOOKS UP TO THE SKY,
SAYING WHO'S THAT CRAZY BOY ABOUT
TO DIE? BEANSTALKER.
BUT HE MIGHT JUST SURPRISE US ALL AND
FLY,
'CAUSE HE'S THE BEANSTALKER,
NOT SOME OTHER GUY.
BEANSTALKER.

                   FARMER
IS HE A MOONWALKER?

                    ALL
NO!

                 FARMER'S WIFE
IS HE A FAST TALKER?

                ANN AND RICHARD
NO! NEITHER OF THE ABOVE.
JUST A BOY THAT WE LOVE.

                    ALL
BEANSTALKER.

                   FARMER
SOMEBODY'S GOT TO BE A HERO,
SOMETIMES THE ONE YOU LEAST SUSPECT.

                 FARMER'S WIFE
ONE DAY THEY'RE NOTHING BUT A ZERO,
NEXT DAY THEY GET IT ALL CORRECT.

                    ALL
AND EVERYBODY LOOKS UP TO THE SKY,
SAYING WHO'S THAT CRAZY BOY ABOUT
TO DIE? BEANSTALKER.

BUT HE MIGHT JUST SURPRISE US ALL AND
FLY,
'CAUSE HE'S THE BEANSTALKER,
NOT SOME OTHER GUY
BRANSTALKER.

STORYTELLER

Back inside the GIANT's kitchen, JACK was sweeping the floor. Suddenly, the GIANTESS entered the kitchen carrying MELODY, who was imprisoned by the strings of a large harp. The GIANTESS placed her on a shelf and said:

GIANTESS

Well, he's heard enough of you for now. I don't see what's so attractive about you anyway, especially when I have such a lovely voice.

STORYTELLER

JACK stopped sweeping and stood frozen, shocked to see MELODY. Noticing this, the GIANTESS spoke to JACK, saying:

GIANTESS

Yes, it's MELODY...now back to work or it's into the oven with you. Wouldn't you be a tasty morsel for the GIANT?

STORYTELLER

JACK went back to sweeping and the GIANTESS walked away, laughing. Again JACK stopped his work to face MELODY and say:

JACK

MELODY, it is I, JACK. We met as I climbed the
beanstalk.

MELODY

Yes, I know. Hello, JACK. You didn't heed my
warning.

JACK

I wanted to see you again.

MELODY

Oh, JACK, look where I've led you. Now you're
imprisoned as I am, and as the Golden Goose is.

JACK

Golden Goose?

MELODY

*Yes. The GIANT has a goose that lays golden eggs.
That's why he's so wealthy.*

JACK

And where did he get such a creature?

MELODY

I've been told that he stole it from a knight.

JACK

What happened to the knight?

MELODY

He made a MAGICIAN put a spell on the knight.
The MAGICIAN wasn't evil like the GIANT. He
tried to make the spell a harmless, short-lived one.

JACK

And was it?

MELODY

Not exactly. You see, the MAGICIAN had a problem, most of his tricks backfired.

JACK

And in the case of the knight?

MELODY

He disappeared in a puff of smoke.

JACK

MELODY, I know that MAGICIAN and I know the knight.

MELODY

You do? How?

JACK

My mother told me about the MAGICIAN. He came to my house. Then he bought our cow for the beans that grew into the beanstalk.

MELODY

Sounds like one of his tricks.

JACK

But he was trying to help me.

MELODY

Like he helped the knight?

JACK

Like he helped my father.

MELODY

You're not saying?

JACK

MELODY, did the knight have a family?

MELODY

A wife and a baby. He wanted to settle down and become a farmer. When he disappeared, and the GIANT stole the goose and they became very poor.

JACK

But they survived! MELODY, the knight was my father, and I believe he's still alive. I must undo the spell. And I must release you.

STORYTELLER

JACK began to try to free her from the harp, which alarmed her. She said:

MELODY

No! If you try to free me from the strings the harp will play and warn the GIANT.

STORYTELLER

JACK was determined. They went back and forth, saying:

JACK

But I can't leave you this way.

MELODY

But there are many like me.

JACK

There are?

MELODY

Yes. Many children of the sky, enslaved by evil spells to serve the GIANT. But he cannot hold us forever.

But how can you hope to be free when the situation
seems hopeless?

MELODY
I AM A SPIRIT BORN TO FLY,
ONE OF THE CHILDREN OF THE SKY.
JUST LIKE A BIRD, I SHOULD BE FREE,
THAT IS THE DREAM SUSTAINING ME.

'THOUGH I'M INSIDE THIS WISPY CLOUD,
ONE DAY I'LL SHED THIS MISTY SHROUD,
WHERE BY A SPELL I AM CONTROLLED,
CHAINED TO THE GIANT'S HARP OF GOLD.

AND STILL I'LL HOPE
FOR A SKY OF BLUE,
I'LL TRY TO COPE
'TIL MY DREAM COMES TRUE.
NOT JUST FOR ME,
NOT JUST FOR YOU,
ALL THE CHILDREN OF THE SKY,
THEIR PARENTS NEVER KNEW.

I AM AN ORPHAN OF THE EARTH,
LOST IN THIS LIMBO SINCE MY BIRTH.
STILL, I'LL BELIEVE ETERNALLY,
ONE DAY I'LL FIND A FAMILY.

ALTHOUGH I SING SUCH DULCET TONES,
INSIDE YOU'LL HEAR A VOICE THAT
MOANS,
LONGING TO CUT THESE BINDING STRINGS,
AND LEAVE THE CAGE AROUND MY
WINGS.

AND STILL I'LL HOPE,
FOR A SKY OF BLUE.
I'LL TRY TO COPE,

'TIL MY DREAM COMES TRUE.
NOT JUST FOR ME,
NOT JUST FOR YOU,
ALL THE CHILDREN OF THE SKY,
THEIR PARENTS NEVER KNEW.

                    JACK
AND STILL I YEARN,
JUST TO TOUCH YOUR FACE.
I'LL TRY TO LEARN,
WHY THESE CLOUDS ERASE,
THE ONES I SEE,
NOT ONLY YOU,
ALL THE CHILDREN OF THE SKY,
LOST OUT THERE IN THE BLUE

THERE WAS A LIGHT ABOVE MY GAZE,
IT WAS A SIGN THAT GOD DISPLAYS.
I'D NEVER KNOW WITHOUT THE CLIMB,
THAT'S BEEN THE ANSWER ALL THROUGH
TIME.

                   MELODY
NOW IT IS TIME TO SAY GOODBYE,
MY IMAGE FADES NOW FROM THE SKY.
JUST LIKE A BIRD WHO WEARS A RING,
WHEN HE COMMANDS, I HAVE TO SING.

                    BOTH
ALL THE CHILDREN OF THE SKY,
LOST OUT THERE IN THE BLUE,
THEIR PARENTS NEVER KNEW.
DO YOU SEE THE CHILDREN OF THE SKY?
SEE THEM WAY UP HIGH?
THEY'RE WATCHING YOU.

                STORYTELLER
*Then, the GIANTESS entered the room with the
room holding the MAGICIAN by the arm. He was*

*dressed in a ridiculous looking Golden Goose outfit.
She admonished JACK and MELODY, saying:*

GIANTESS
JACK! Mind your own business and get back to
work. And you, MELODY, save your voice! The
master might want to hear more later, although I don't
know why...And don't disturb our new Golden Goose.

STORYTELLER
*Then, she left the room in a huff. After that,
MELODY spoke directly to the Golden
Goose, who was really the MAGICIAN.*

MELODY
But are you also a Golden Goose?

MAGICIAN

Sort of. The GIANT's Golden Goose....

JACK
You! You're the MAGICIAN,

MELODY
You mean the knight's Golden Goose.

MAGICIAN

Whatever....the goose has sort of stopped cooperating
with the GIANT. He forced me to conjure up a new
goose.

JACK

Don't tell me...flowers?

MAGICIAN

No, but the trick did backfire. I turned into a Golden
Goose. And I must say, I'm enjoying it.

SO, LIFE ISN'T FAIR...
WELL, WHAT CAN I SAY?
IF YOU WORK ALL YEAR,
WHILE I GET TO PLAY?

I JUST HAVE A GIFT,
APART FROM THE REST.
JUST ONE LITTLE LIFT,
WILL FEATHER MY NEST.

LOUNGING IN MY GOWN,
COZY IN MY DOWN,
NOT JUST ANOTHER PIECE OF POULTRY,
A BIRD OF RENOWN.

THE PRIDE AND JOY OF THE MASTER,
I LIKE IT BEST WHEN HE BEGS.
MY LIFE WOULD BE A DISASTER,
LUCKY THING HE NEEDS THE EGGS.

NO, LIFE ISN'T FAIR,
NOT FAIR FOR A FOWL,
WHEN THE MASTER SPEAKS,
TO ME, WITH A SCOWL.
BUT I'D NEVER TEASE,
I WOULDN'T WITHHOLD,
BUT IF HE SAYS 'PLEASE,'

THEN HE GETS THE GOLD.

THREATENING ABUSE?
THERE'S REALLY NO USE.
NO ONE'S GOING TO KILL A FORTUNE,
OR A GOLDEN GOOSE.

MAGICIAN
THE PRIDE AND JOY OF THE MASTER,
I LIKE IT BEST WHEN HE BEGS,
MY LIFE WOULD BE A DISASTER,
LUCKY THING HE NEEDS THE EGGS.

JACK
THERE WILL COME A DAY,
WHEN YOU CAN'T PERFORM.
YOU WON'T PAY YOUR WAY,
YOU'LL HAVE TO CONFORM.

MAGICIAN
WELL, UNTIL I FAIL
I'LL REMAIN OBTUSE,
THEN PICK UP MY TAIL,
AND LET AN EGG LOOSE.

LINGERING WITH DOUBT,
HE'LL KEEP ME ABOUT,
OR LEAVE HIMSELF TO ALWAYS WONDER,
DID THE LAST COME OUT?

THE PRIDE AND JOY OF THE MASTER,
I LIKE IT BEST WHEN HE BEGS,
MY LIFE WOULD BE A DISASTER,
LUCKY THING HE NEEDS,
LOVE IT WHEN HE PLEADS,
LUCKY THING HE NEEDS THE EGGS.

STORYTELLER
*Then JACK spoke to the GOLDEN GOOSE/MAGICIAN
again.*

JACK
MAGICIAN, once you said you wanted to help
me...

MAGICIAN
And I did, with those magic beans.

JACK
(Sarcastically.)
You mean the beanstalk was a career ladder. It led
to this wonderful sweeping job.

MAGICIAN
Oh, sorry about that.

JACK
If you're really sorry, help me.

MAGICIAN
How can I help?

JACK
(Pointing to MELODY.)
Can you free her without warning the GIANT?

MELODY
JACK, it's too risky...

JACK
We'll never be free unless we take some risks.

MAGICIAN
Let me try.

JACK
Before you do, where is the real Golden Goose?

MAGICIAN
The GIANT keeps her in this cage.

STORYTELLER
The MAGICIAN reached down and produced a cage with the GOOSE in it and handed it to JACK. Then he said:

JACK
Thank you. Now, please free MELODY.

STORYTELLER
The MAGICIAN waved his wand and the harp sounded loudly. JACK took MELODY by the hand and she was free. As he ran away with MELODY and the cage with the Golden Goose, the angry GIANT burst in and started chasing JACK around the house, saying:

GIANT
DID YOU REALLY HAVE THE NERVE
TO STEAL MY GOLD?
WELL, YOU NEVER DID DESERVE,
TO BE SO BOLD.

AH, BUT NOW YOU'D BETTER DUCK,
YOU'D BETTER RUN,
BECAUSE YOU'VE RUN OUT OF LUCK
YOU'VE HAD YOUR FUN.

SMALL MAN,
I'M GONNA GET YOU,
I'M GONNA MAKE YOU PAY.
SMALL MAN,
I WON'T FORGET YOU,
OR LET YOU GET AWAY,
SMALL MAN.

THOSE WITH MONEY WHO ARE BIG
GET ALL THE TOYS.
I'M JUST NOT IN THE SAME LEAGUE
WITH LITTLE BOYS.

IF I'M STRONG AND YOU'RE WEAK,
WHAT ARE YOU WORTH?

JACK
YOU'LL FIND OUT WHEN THE MEEK,
HAVE CLAIMED THE EARTH.

TALL MAN,
YOU'LL NEVER GET ME,
AND I'LL DO WHAT I MUST.
TALL MAN.
I WILL BE SET FREE,
BECAUSE MY CAUSE IS JUST.
TALL MAN.

GIANT

SMALL MAN,
I'M GONNA GET YOU,
I'M GONNA MAKE YOU PAY.
SMALL MAN,
I WON'T FORGET YOU,
OR LET YOU GET AWAY,
SMALL MAN. SMALL MAN!

STORYTELLER

JACK and MELODY eluded the GIANT, ran out of the house and across the clouds. They began to climb down the beanstalk. The GIANT followed in hot pursuit, clumsily climbing down the beanstalk above them. He wasn't an experienced climber, since he normally walked slowly to the land below on a large mountain. The GIANT began to tire and lose his grip on the branches. All in an instant, his life passed before his eyes and he expressed his regrets, saying:

GIANT

MY LIFE WAS WASTED ALL FOR GREED,
I WANTED THINGS I DIDN'T NEED.
FOR GOLD A SOUL CAN NEVER SAVE,
I TOOK AND TOOK, BUT NEVER GAVE.

STORYTELLER

The people below gasped as the GIANT began falling slowly through the vines of the beanstalk.

GIANT
TANGLED IN VINES OF MY OWN LIES,
TRAPPED AS THE HUMAN SPIRIT FLIES,
MY MUSCLES NEVER GAVE ME STRENGTH
OR CHARACTER FOR ALL THEIR LENGTH.

AND NOW I SEE THE PLACE BELOW,
WHERE I AM SOON TO FACE THE MUD,
IN THE DARK MOMENT THAT WE KNOW,
HOW WE HAVE SPILLED OUR BROTHER'S
BLOOD,

THE DAY COMES WHEN WE LOSE IT ALL,
AND THAT IS THE DAY OF THE FALL.

STORYTELLER
The GIANT fell further, then stopped, trapped on the beanstalk, unable to climb to the top or bottom before JACK chopped it down. By the time the GIANT was halfway down the beanstalk, which still stood beside the farmhouse, JACK and MELODY reached the ground. As ANN and MELODY looked on, JACK chopped at the beanstalk with an ax. ANN shouted:

ANN
Look out!

GIANT
SOMEHOW IT SUDDENLY SEEMS LATE,
THE BRANCHES BREAK BENEATH MY WEIGHT,
THE BURDEN OF SO MANY YEARS
OF STEALING SMILES AND CAUSING
TEARS.

STORYTELLER

As the GIANT fell with the beanstalk, the people below ran for cover. They heard a loud thud and then turn to see a large deep crater and then they speak:

JACK

Look at the size of that hole!

ANN

That hole is now the GIANT'S grave.

STORYTELLER

Then another large object fell and MELODY spoke, saying:

MELODY

Look out, it's the GIANTESS!

STORYTELLER

They heard another thud, to which they responded.

JACK

Two holes.

ANN

Two dead GIANTS! At last the shadow is gone. Our crops will live again.

MELODY

Too bad...

JACK AND ANN

Too bad?

MELODY

About the MAGICIAN...with the beanstalk gone, and the GIANTS, too, he's stranded up in the castle with no way down.

STORYTELLER
*But the MAGICIAN landed on the farm among them
in his golden goose costume, with his wings spread,
and I said:*

MAGICIAN
This goose trick came in handy.

ANN, JACK and MELODY patted the MAGICIAN
on the back and welcome him. He then shed his
goose costume and said:

MAGICIAN
I finally mastered magic. I will now produce...
flowers!

STORYTELLER
*The MAGICIAN pulled flowers from my pocket. The
people replied:*

ANN
You've mastered a better trick

JACK
Yes. You got us to believe in ourselves. That's how
I defeated the GIANT.

STORYTELLER
*Then the FARMER and the FARMER's WIFE ran to
embrace MELODY, saying:*

FARMER
And that's how we got our daughter back.

MELODY
Mother! Father!

FARMER'S WIFE
Oh, I missed you so. We worried so.

MELODY

And I missed you.

FARMER

But now we're a family again.

STORYTELLER

JACK and ANN looked at each other sadly. MELODY turned to JACK as she freed herself from the harp and said:

MELODY

JACK, look! The spell is broken! I'm free! Oh, JACK, don't you see what this means?

STORYTELLER

Dejected, then elated as he thought over the situation through, JACK said:

JACK

No, wait a minute. If the spell is broken, and you're no longer bound by a harp...

MAGICIAN

And I'm no longer trapped in the feathers of a goose...and, look... our friend is laying eggs again.

JACK

Then...

STORYTELLER

Suddenly, RICHARD appeared, not as a phantom, but as a knight, a husband and a father.

MAGICIAN
Nothing's too much to hope for if you believe in
yourself, remember?

JACK
ONCE UPON A TIME THERE WAS A MAN,
AND HE WATCHED WHILE I WAS SLEEPING,
I KNOW HE WATCHED OVER ME AND
SMILED,
I WAS SAFELY IN HIS KEEPING.

STORYTELLER
RICHARD and ANN and JACK embraced and said:

RICHARD
My son...My wife...

IN A FAIRY TALE I WAS A KNIGHT,
UPON LOVE I'VE BEEN DEPENDING.
IT SUSTAINED ME THROUGH AND ENDLESS
NIGHT,
LED ME TO A HAPPY ENDING.

ALL
AND NOW A LIGHT WILL SHINE ACROSS THE LAND,
AND WE'LL BUILD MOUNTAINS OUT OF DREAMS
AND SAND,
THEN, AS COLORS SPARKLE ACROSS THE PLAIN,
WE'LL HAVE OUR ONCE UPON A TIME AGAIN.

RICHARD opened the cage and let the Golden Goose fly free. Just then all the children of the sky began to float down to land softly on the countryside, where they were happily reunited with their parents. Everyone came together and said:

ALL
SOMEBODY'S GOT TO ASK THE QUESTION,
SOMEBODY'S GOT TO TAKE A STAND,
SOMEBODY'S GOT TO HAVE AN ANSWER,
SOMEBODY'S GOT TO RAISE A HAND.

SOMEBODY'S STARTING AT THE BOTTOM,
ONE DAY WHO'S BOUND TO REACH THE
TOP, SOMEBODY'S PICKING UP MOMENTUM,
SOMEBODY NO ONE'S GOING TO STOP.

SOMEBODY'S GOT TO BE A WINNER,
SOMEBODY ELSE WILL HAVE TO LOSE.
SOMEBODY'S GOT THE LUCKY NUMBER,
AND THE WORLD IS FILLED WITH NUMBER
TWOS.

SOMEBODY'S GOT TO FACE THE GIANT,
ONE DAY WHO'S BOUND TO BRING HIM DOWN.
IT'S JUST LIKE DAVID AND GOLIATH,
SAME STORY IN A DIFFERENT TOWN.

AND EVERYONE LOOKS UP TO THE SKY,
SAYING WHO'S THAT CRAZY BOY ABOUT
TO DIE?
BEANSTALKER.
BUT HE JUST MIGHT SURPRISE US ALL AND
FLY,
'CAUSE HE'S THE BEANSTALKER,
NOT SOME OTHER GUY.
BEANSTALKER.

SOMEBODY'S GOT TO HAVE THE COURAGE
THAT GROWS FROM CONQUERING A FEAR,
SOMEBODY MUST BELIEVE IN SOMETHING,
AND RECOGNIZE IT WHEN IT'S THERE.

STORYTELLER
JACK raised his hand and everyone stood still in silence. Then JACK turned to the MAGICIAN and said:

JACK
I just have one question. If you're not really a goose, where to the golden eggs come from?

MAGICIAN
Chickens and gold paint, but don't tell the GIANT.

STORYTELLER
And they all laughed. Then JACK said:

JACK
SOMEBODY'S GOT TO BE A LONER,
BUT NO ONE DOES IT ALONE.

MAGICIAN
TOGETHER WE CAN CLIMB FOREVER,

GIANT
DIVIDED, WE FALL LIKE A STONE.

FARMER
IS HE A MOONWALKER?

FULL COMPANY
NO!

FARMER'S WIFE
IS HE A FAST TALKER?

ANN and RICHARD
NO! NEITHER OF THE ABOVE,
JUST A BOY THAT WE LOVE.

FULL COMPANY
BEANSTALKER. BEANSTALKER. BEANSTALKER.

Author, lyricist, and playwright, Edward Kenny

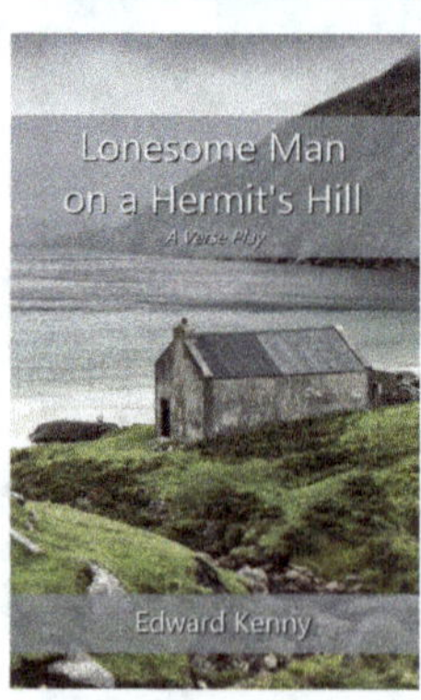

About the Author

Other books by Edward Kenny include *Bluebird Songs – Volumes I, II* and *III*, which contain lyrics and poems, along with the following librettos/verse plays: *Lonesome Man on Hermit's Hill* and *The Outlaw*. Ed has written over 1,500 song lyrics and the book and lyrics for ten musicals. He first entered the Broadway scene in 1982, when *Valhalla,* a musical he co-wrote with his longtime collaborator, composer/arranger, Val Angrosini, received a first-class option. Material from the show was aired on television in conjunction with the *Hempkompst* expedition, a recreated Viking dragon ship which sailed from New York Harbor to Oslo, Norway. "*Valhalla*" was previewed by *Broadway Tomorrow Musical Theatre*, and was selected as a finalist in the New York Drama League Grants Competition. The New York Foundation for the Arts awarded a grant to present *"Valhalla"* as a performance art work.

"The World Goes On," a song from *Valhalla*, was aired on WGBB 1240, where Val and Ed were interviewed. At that time, two songs that they had written to commemorate the tragic events of September 11, 2001 were played, along with other original material.

Two additional musicals by this writing team, *Goodnight St. Petersburg* and *Straight to the Ace,* were also previewed by Broadway tomorrow. Material from the shows was also aired on the New York City cable television talk/variety show *What's Going On,* where Val and Ed appeared as guests.

Straight to the Ace was nominated for the *Dramatists Guild* musical theatre program. It was also nominated by the *American Academy of Arts and Letters* for the *Harold Prince Musical Theatre* program. *Purple Cow Playhouse, Ltd.* presented the show under a grant from the New York State Council on the Arts. *Ace* was also presented in *New York City*.

The Angrosini/Kenny collaboration began in 1979. The two have penned hundreds of songs which have been performed by Val's original bands at *The Right Track Inn*, *Paulson's*, *Catch a Rising Star*, *The Brokerage*, and other metropolitan area clubs, and recently, throughout central Florida. Their theme song for the group *Amethyst* was aired on television commercials. Val and Ed both received the Oliver Award from Broadway Tomorrow Musical Theatre.

Mission IV, an album by the internationally acclaimed Markus Escher and The Bowmen, includes a song with lyrics by Ed, entitled *"Broken Man."*

Ed and composer, Al Grilli, were finalist in the Babylon Citizens' Council on the Arts (BACCA) annual songwriting competition. Their original songs were aired on WUSB radio, and one of Ed's songs was played on the television series *PM Magazine*. His lyrics have been published in the *Bard's Annual*, the *Suffolk County Poetry Review*, *Rhyme and Punishment*, *Long Island Haunts* and *Harmonic Verse*.

He studied poetry and lyric writing while attaining his Bachelor's Degree at Adelphi University.